Chris Bradford

BULLET CATCHER

SNIPER

With illustrations by
Nelson Evergreen

Barrington Stoke

For more information on Chris and his books visit:
www.chrisbradford.co.uk

First published in 2016 in Great Britain by
Barrington Stoke Ltd
18 Walker Street, Edinburgh, EH3 7LP

www.barringtonstoke.co.uk

Text © 2016 Chris Bradford
Illustrations © 2016 Nelson Evergreen

A CIP catalogue record for this book is available
from the British Library upon request

ISBN: 978-1-78112-446-8

Printed in China by Leo

Warning: Do not attempt any of the techniques described within the book. These
can be highly dangerous and result in fatal injuries. The author and publisher take
no responsibility for any injuries resulting from attempting these techniques.

For Thomas Dyson,
 A bulletproof super-fan!

CONTENTS

CHAPTER 1
GLINT OF SUNLIGHT

The Near Future

Troy waited like a patient boyfriend as Pandora browsed the racks of glamorous dresses. But he had little hope that he would ever be the sweetheart of this beauty with her raven hair and honey skin. Pandora was the daughter of Carlos Lomez, the Mayor of Terminus City and the Chairman of the all-powerful Council. She was way out of Troy's league.

His job was to protect her.

Troy's gaze swept round the designer fashion store. Among the customers he spotted an ice-blonde girl. She appeared to be looking at a silk top. In fact, her sharp blue eyes were watching the other shoppers.

Kasia was a bulletcatcher like Troy, assigned to guard Pandora.

Outside the shop a large boy loitered, with arms like blocks of black granite. That was Lennox – the muscle on their team.

There was no sign of any threat. Even so Troy felt on edge. He'd hated shopping malls ever since his parents were killed in one in a terrorist attack. Over a year had passed, but the grief still burned like acid in his gut.

As he kept a lookout for danger, Troy caught sight of his own reflection in a mirror. Tall and pale with sandy cropped hair, he looked a little gawky. But he was no longer the scrawny boy he once was . After months of intensive bulletcatcher training, his body was stronger and more defined.

"What do you think of this one?" Pandora asked. She held a ruby red dress against her slim figure.

Troy stared at her. His confidence was growing, but he was still tongue-tied when it came to girls. Especially one as pretty as Pandora. "Ermm ... very nice," he said.

Pandora smiled. "You've said that about *all* the clothes I've shown you."

She paid for the dress and several other items, then strolled out of the store. Lennox walked ahead and took 'point'. Troy kept close on Pandora's right. Kasia followed behind on their left. In this way, Pandora was protected from all sides.

"Heading to north exit," Kasia whispered into her throat mic.

Troy heard a reply in their earpieces from Joe, their comms contact at SPEAR HQ. "Transport ETA one minute," Joe said.

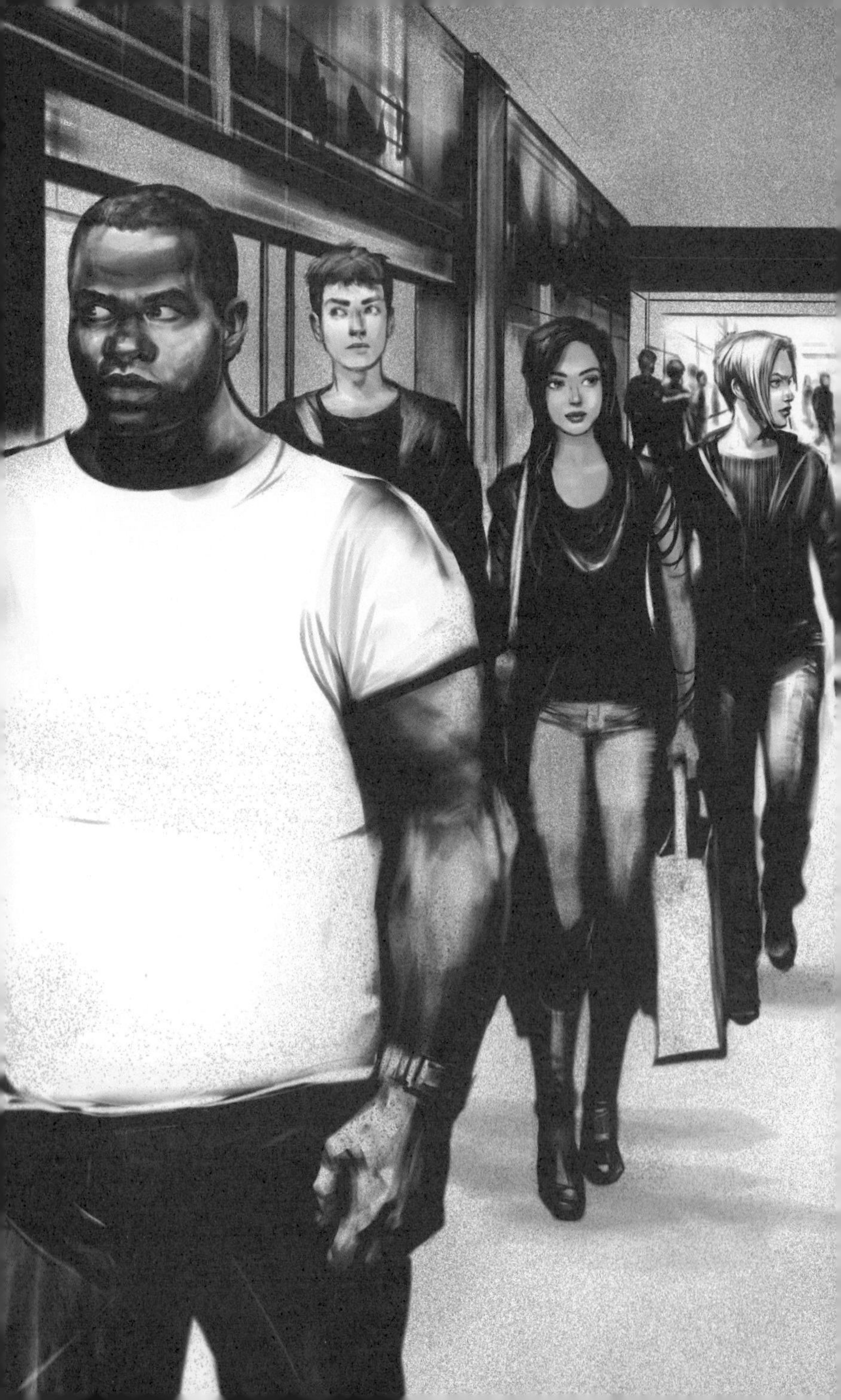

Troy's nerves grew worse. Whenever a VIP got in or out of a vehicle, they were vulnerable. This was the moment they were most exposed to a potential attack.

Pandora and her bulletcatchers reached the exit as the limo pulled up to the kerb outside.

The mall's glass doors slid open. Lennox stepped onto the street and did a quick scan. His eyes lingered on a man talking into a mobile before he gave the all-clear.

Troy escorted Pandora across the pavement. Lennox opened the limo's rear door. As Troy guided Pandora towards it, his eyes darted everywhere for threats. The man with the mobile had finished his call and was walking towards them. Kasia stepped forward and blocked his path. The man may have been innocent, but they couldn't take any chances.

Pandora was totally unaware of the threat as she slipped into the back seat with her shopping bags.

"Well, that was easy," Lennox said with a grin. He had begun to close the door when the limo's front tyre burst. "Oh hell!" he said. "We've got a flat –"

Troy looked up. His eyes were drawn by a glint of sunlight from the roof of a building further along the street. Suddenly Lennox gave a wounded cry and keeled over.

At that moment, Pandora climbed back out. "I've forgotten my purse," she said.

"No!" Troy cried as she left the safety of the vehicle.

Troy leaped forward to cover Pandora with his body. He felt a bullet strike his back. Then another. The impacts knocked the air from his lungs. He hit the pavement hard.

A second later, Pandora fell beside him. A bullet in her head.

CHAPTER 2
BULLET EARS

Troy stared into Pandora's dead eyes. Despair welled up in him. He'd *failed* to protect her.

Pandora's face flickered. Then blinked out.

The street scene and limo also vanished to reveal a huge round room with a domed roof. The walls glowed soft white and a faint hum could be heard. The Reactor Room simulation was over.

Troy recovered his breath then got to his feet. He entered the control room with Kasia and a dazed Lennox.

"Lucky you're bulletproof," Azumi said to Troy. Her long black hair was tied into a ponytail, and her eyes were hidden behind a pair of sunglasses.

"Yeah, *he's* bulletproof," Lennox moaned. He rubbed the back of his head where one of the rubber bullets had hit him. "But I'm not!"

"You're super-strong. You can take it." Kasia laughed.

Lennox narrowed his eyes at her. "How come you didn't get shot?"

"Reflex, baby, Reflex," she replied with a wink.

Each of the team had been signed up by SPEAR – a top secret protection agency – because of their unique talents. Troy was bulletproof. Lennox had the Hercules gene that made him 50% stronger than even the strongest adult. Azumi had Blindsight that allowed her to glimpse into the future and warn of danger. Kasia's Reflex talent meant she could react six times faster than any normal human.

Before Lennox could sit down, Kasia claimed the only other chair in the room.

"Too slow!" She laughed as she propped her feet on the control desk and leaned back.

Joe tutted and pushed her feet off so he could study the screen's read-outs. He was a skinny boy with square glasses that suited a tech-head.

"So how did we do?" Kasia asked as she put her feet back on the desk.

Joe looked up at her and frowned. "Your VIP is dead. You failed."

"We know *that*," Kasia replied breezily. "But did we get any points?"

"Points are pointless if your VIP is killed," Joe said. Still, he examined the read-out. "The team was scoring well at first. 98% for surveillance skills in the clothes store. 95% for the walking drill. 62% for street observation. 30% for transfer into the limo –"

"Why the sudden drop in our scores?" Troy asked.

"None of you looked *up* as you moved the VIP from the mall to the limo. You all focused on the obvious threat – the man in the street. Then you dropped your guard as soon as Pandora was in the car. So you missed the sniper on the roof."

Troy recalled the glint of sunlight. That must have been from the scope on the sniper's rifle!

"But how are we supposed to spot a sniper?" Lennox complained.

"You can't," Joe replied. "That's what makes them so deadly."

Lennox threw his hands up in the air. "So we had no chance!"

"Not really," Joe said. "Snipers use camouflage, choose a firing position with care and often attack from long distances. It's only *after* a sniper has taken their first shot that you have any chance of locating them. Of course, it's often too late by then."

"Are you saying we can't *ever* stop a sniper?" Kasia asked.

Joe pulled up an image on the computer screen of a large mast with an array of sensors. "This is a Boomerang device. A military system that uses microphones to calculate the sniper's position from the muzzle blast and the bullet's sonic shock-wave. But the device needs to be mounted to a vehicle, costs a lot and weighs a ton. The other option is a dog."

"Really?" Azumi said. She looked thoughtful.

Joe nodded. "Trained dogs can work out the direction of the sniper from the sound of the bullet. In the Vietnam War one famous dog located over one hundred enemy snipers by lying down with his head pointed at the origin of the gunshot. They nicknamed him Bullet Ears."

"Shame none of us are dogs, huh?" Lennox said.

"Speak for yourself," Kasia joked. "You smell like one!"

Lennox wrinkled his nose in mock offence. "If that's the case, then you'd be a Husky! And Azumi would be a Pekingese."

"I'm from Japan, not China, Dog-breath!" Azumi shot back.

"Whatever," Lennox said with a shrug. "Troy's from Poland and he'd still be a tiny Shih Tzu!"

"That's lame, Lennox," Troy replied. He turned to Joe. "So what are our best tactics to deal with a sniper?"

"Obviously if you're still alive, take cover," Joe replied. "Next, escape the kill-zone as fast as you can. But the best defence is to prevent it ever happening. A security team should sweep the area in advance. Then you should post guards on all rooftops and tall buildings. The more eyes and ears the better. But that takes a lot of resources, both in terms of money and manpower."

Troy shook his head in amazement. "How do you know all this?" he asked.

Joe gave him a puzzled look. "I've told you before, I retain 98% of everything I see and read thanks to my –"

Troy held up a hand and smiled. "Yeah, I know, your autistic superpowers!"

The door to the control room slid open and a woman appeared. She had spiked white hair and a silver-grey suit. Medusa was the head of SPEAR and the severe look on her face told them she had bad news.

"The sniper's struck again."

CHAPTER 3
THE JUDGE

A short woman with a brown bob and sturdy shoes strode out of the new hospital. As she waved goodbye to the crowd, her body jerked and she fell to the ground. Blood spread in a large red pool around her head.

Troy watched the replay of the attack in mute horror. The other bulletcatchers also sat stunned in the large round briefing chamber as the hologram desk zoomed in on the scene.

"Anna Kerner is the *third* member of the Council to be killed in as many months," the newsreader said. "It seems Terminus City is no longer safe for anyone."

The camera switched to the TV studio, where the blonde newsreader sat with the stern-faced Head of Council Security.

"Are your security forces failing us, Commander Hanz?" the newsreader asked.

"Of course not!" the commander snapped. "For the hospital's opening ceremony, we had police stationed for a three-block radius."

He stabbed a finger at the area lit up in green on a digital map of the city.

"The sniper was beyond this zone, hidden in a radio tower."

A red dot glowed near the edge of the map.

"Only one in a million could have made such a shot," the commander said. "No one could have foreseen or prevented such an attack. We're up against a professional sniper. We suspect he's ex-elite forces."

With a grim nod the newsreader turned to the camera. "This is a worrying development in our battle against the terrorists. Once again the Army of Freedom have claimed responsibility for this latest attack in an online video by their leader, The Judge."

The newscast switched to a man in a robe and a Janus mask – a half black, half white face that was both smiling and crying.

"I am your judge, jury and executioner," the masked man said in a rasping voice. "Terminus City is immoral. The Council is corrupt. The Mayor is a thief and liar."

He held up a small wooden hammer to the camera. "The sentence is death!"

He brought the hammer down onto its wooden block with a sharp *crack*.

The Judge went on. "My Army of Freedom will tear this city down and rebuild it in the name of God." He turned his head so only the smile showed. "Be faithful and you will live."

Then he twisted to show the single black tear on the other side. "But all non-believers and sinners will die."

Troy's stomach knotted in anger at The Judge's words. His parents *hadn't* been non-believers or sinners. They were good people. Innocent. Just living their lives. Their only crime was to be shopping at the time of the mall attack when these terrorists gunned them down in cold blood.

Their deaths were the reason Troy was now a bulletcatcher.

He'd never imagined or wanted to be a bodyguard. He wasn't a natural hero – not like Kasia. But he'd been forced into the role by all that had happened. And, having watched The Judge's video, Troy was more determined than

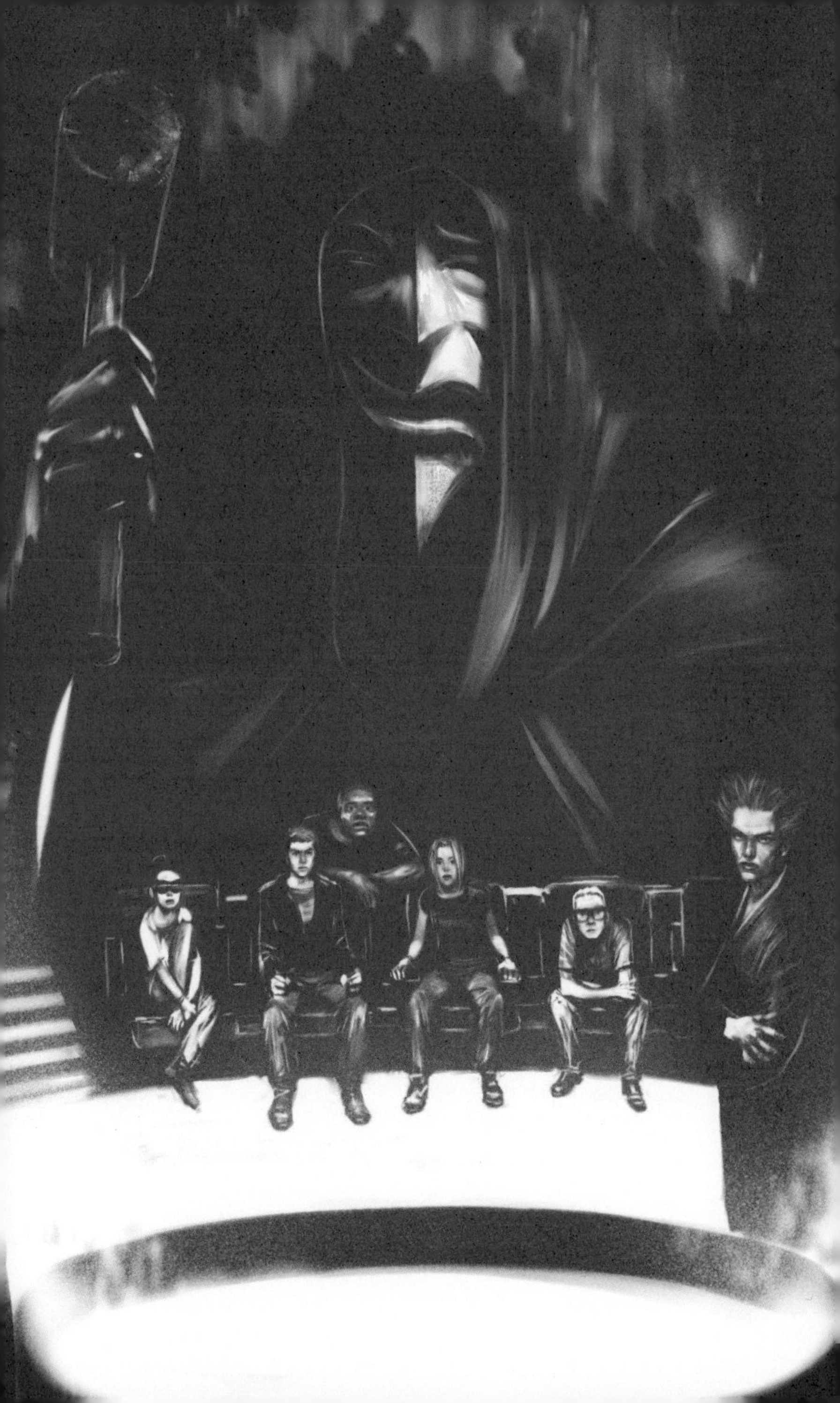

ever to stop the terrorists and their insane crusade.

The video was followed by a news clip of a tanned man with dark eyebrows, a square jaw and silver-grey hair. The calm and determined face of Mayor Lomez.

"We will *not* be terrorised by the A.F.," the Mayor said, and he pounded a fist on his lectern. "The Judge's threats do not scare me. And they should not scare you. Together we will Fight Against Fear."

The mayor pointed to a banner with the words *Fight Against Fear* etched on a shield.

"The Council has already agreed tighter security measures," Mayor Lomez went on. "One hundred more city drones will fly the skies. Thirty more armed police units will patrol the streets. Online surveillance will be extended. There'll be no rock, roof or computer these terrorists can hide behind."

He stared direct into the camera lens. "As your mayor, I promise to keep this city safe from these faceless terrorists."

Medusa switched off the hologram desk and turned to Troy and the others.

"Well, that speech should guarantee him another four years as mayor," she said, then raised a thin eyebrow. "Which means he and his daughter will continue to be the prime target for the A.F. Your role as bulletcatchers is more vital than ever."

CHAPTER 4
ZANSHIN ZONE

"*I'm dying!*" Troy gasped.

"QUIT MOANING!" Apollo barked. Their fitness and combat instructor was a six-foot-two mountain of bad-tempered muscle and the only help he gave Troy was to shout, "PAIN IS TEMPORARY!"

Troy lugged the heavy medicine ball to the far end of the gym for the tenth time. His legs trembled beneath him, his arms ached and his heart threatened to burst out of his ribs. Even Fit Pills were no help under training this intense.

"Next station!" Apollo ordered.

Troy dropped the medicine ball with a *thud*, staggered across to a mat and began to do a combination of press-ups, star jumps and burpees. Lennox jogged past him with Joe on his back. He was sweating buckets.

"I'm melting," Lennox complained as he completed another circuit of the gym.

"Sweat is just your fat crying!" Apollo replied, and made as if to kick him in the rear. "Get moving!"

Lennox stumbled on. When someone as strong as Lennox was struggling, Troy realised he had little chance. With every star jump he was feeling more and more light-headed.

"Your talents may give you the edge in an attack, but they won't guarantee your VIP's survival ... or your own!" Apollo said as he added extra weight to Kasia's bench press. "No point having superpowers, if you're not in the right place at the right time. That's why you must be fighting fit!'

Then he increased the resistance on Azumi's cycling machine and shouted at her to go faster.

"There are three factors that determine your speed to an attack situation," Apollo explained. "Reaction, Response and Rapidity. The Reactor Room can improve Reaction and Response times. But only hard work in the gym will improve Rapidity. This is how swift your muscles contract, how quick your counter punch is, and how fast your body moves out of the way of danger."

Without warning Apollo swung a sledgehammer fist at Troy and caught him in the gut. Troy dropped to the mat, where he fought for breath.

"Troy, you may be able to stop a bullet, but you couldn't stop my fist!" Apollo snarled with a disappointed shake of his bald head.

Tears of pain stung Troy's eyes. *"Why ... did you ... hit me?"* he groaned.

Apollo smiled. "I've just taught you a very valuable lesson. Action beats reaction every single time. Don't just stand there and wait for someone to hit you – *move*."

"But ..." Troy gasped, "how could I know you'd punch me?"

Apollo jerked him to his feet. "You should have been in the Zanshin Zone."

"Zanshin?" Kasia asked. She parked her weights and sat up on the bench with a puzzled frown.

Apollo rolled his eyes. "Azumi, educate these fools."

Azumi stopped cycling. "Zanshin ... refers to a warrior's awareness," she panted. "It literally means *remaining mind*."

"And, as bulletcatchers, you need to be mindful at all times," Apollo said. "Mindful of your potential enemies and surroundings. There's an old samurai warrior saying – *When the battle is over, keep one hand on your sword.*"

"But I don't have a sword," Lennox pointed out as he lowered Joe to the ground.

"Why am I not surprised *you* don't understand?" Apollo growled. "The saying reminds you to stay alert at the end of any combat. It's natural to think the danger is over then – when in reality, it's often not."

All of a sudden Apollo pulled out a handgun and aimed it at Troy's head.

This time Troy did react. For the past month their instructor had been drilling them in gun-disarming techniques until they were second nature. Troy slammed one hand against the gun's barrel and chopped the other into Apollo's wrist, breaking his instructor's grip on the weapon.

The gun still went off, but the bullet missed Troy.

"Good reactions, Troy," Apollo said with a nod of approval. "Shame you killed Kasia in the process."

Troy turned to see Kasia fuming at him, with her ice-blue eyes ablaze. The paintball bullet had plastered her snow-white skin and platinum-blonde hair bright red.

"Sorry," he said with a sheepish grin.

CHAPTER 5
FUNFAIR

"Step up! Test your strength!" the showman called. He beckoned to Troy and the others to try the High Striker.

Pandora had been invited to the city's annual summer funfair by Jeff, the son of Councillor Drayton. The whole family was there. The boy's father was proudly wearing a straw panama hat and was accompanied by several armed bodyguards in black combat gear.

Compared to these hulking security men, Troy and the other bulletcatchers could walk alongside Pandora undetected. No different to the other kids enjoying the old-fashioned funfair.

There were bumper cars, merry-go-rounds, a helter-skelter, a big wheel, side stalls, candy floss and swarms of kids screaming in delight on the thrill-rides. With all the distractions, lights and noise, it was a nightmare location to protect someone.

"Come on! Let's sort the men from the boys!" the showman challenged. "Who's going to impress this pretty little lady here?" He shot a wink at Pandora.

Jeff stepped forward, handed the showman a credit and picked up the wooden mallet. He flicked his mop of ash-blond hair from his eyes, then said to Pandora, "Check this out."

Jeff swung the mallet down hard onto the striker pad. The puck flew up the tower ... but stopped short of the bell.

"Better luck next time!" the showman said with a toothy grin. "Want to try again?"

"Nah," Jeff said. Troy could tell by the boy's sulky tone that he was annoyed at failing in front of Pandora.

"How about you, big man?" the showman said to Lennox.

Lennox shrugged. "OK."

He took the mallet in one hand and hit the striker with no more effort than if he were swatting a fly. The puck shot up like a rocket and the bell rang out.

The showman's jaw fell open in shock. "We've a real-life superman here!"

"Impressive," Pandora said. She smiled at Lennox as he claimed his prize of a furry toy gorilla.

Jeff scowled. "Well, he's got a lot more weight behind him, hasn't he?"

For a moment Lennox looked like he might use the mallet on Jeff.

"How about a different game?" Kasia suggested to defuse the tension. She guided the group towards a side stall.

"Yeah," Jeff said, regaining his confidence. "I'll win you a teddy bear, Pandora."

Jeff pushed into the crowd and headed for the shooting gallery. Troy wasn't warming to the boy. Jeff was rude, arrogant, brash and didn't seem to like Troy standing so close to Pandora all the time.

"Aren't you having a go?" Pandora asked Troy.

Troy shook his head. He couldn't allow himself to become distracted. He had to stay in the Zanshin Zone and keep an eye out for danger.

"Scared of guns, are we?" Jeff teased Troy as he paid the operator.

"I'll have a go," Azumi volunteered.

The operator handed her the rifle. "Ladies first," he said.

"Is this a good idea?" Lennox whispered to Troy. "Giving her a loaded weapon!"

Azumi seemed unfazed by the challenge. She pointed the rifle down the range at the tower of six tin cans on a shelf. She clicked her tongue once then pulled the trigger.

The top can flew off. Troy and Lennox exchanged astonished looks.

Another tongue click, a gunshot and the second can toppled.

As the third can went flying, Jeff asked Joe, "What's with the click?"

"Azumi is blind," Joe replied. "The click helps her echo-locate the target."

Jeff narrowed his eyes at Joe as Azumi shot a fourth can off. "You're pulling my leg."

"No, I'm not," Joe replied with a frown. "My hands are in my pockets."

Jeff looked at Joe as if he was deeply weird, then turned back to the shooting gallery. Azumi had missed the last two cans.

"Aww, unlucky," the operator said with a half-hearted shrug as he re-set the cans.

"Something's wrong," Azumi said. There was a frown on her face.

"Yeah, the sights on these are usually off," Jeff replied as he took the rifle from her. "You have to compensate."

Jeff raised the rifle and took careful aim. As he fired away, Troy couldn't deny he was an excellent shot. Jeff hit each can dead-centre and they pinged off the shelf like shooting stars. When the last can went flying, he punched the air and shouted, "Beat that!"

The operator reluctantly handed over a super-sized teddy bear clutching a red heart. Jeff presented the prize to Pandora with a smug smile.

"Thanks," she said, and hugged the bear to her chest.

"Sharpest shooter in Terminus City!" Jeff boasted. He closed one eye and took aim with the gun at his father, who was buying a stick of candy floss for his little sister. "I reckon I could knock that daft hat off his head from here."

"Something's definitely wrong," Azumi repeated as Jeff made a shooting sound. But not only did his father's hat go flying, his father

dropped to the ground. Blood spurted from a
bullet wound in his neck.

Jeff's face went pale. "But I didn't even pull
the trigger!" he cried.

Troy knew in an instant Jeff *wasn't* to
blame.

"CODE RED!" he shouted. "SNIPER!"

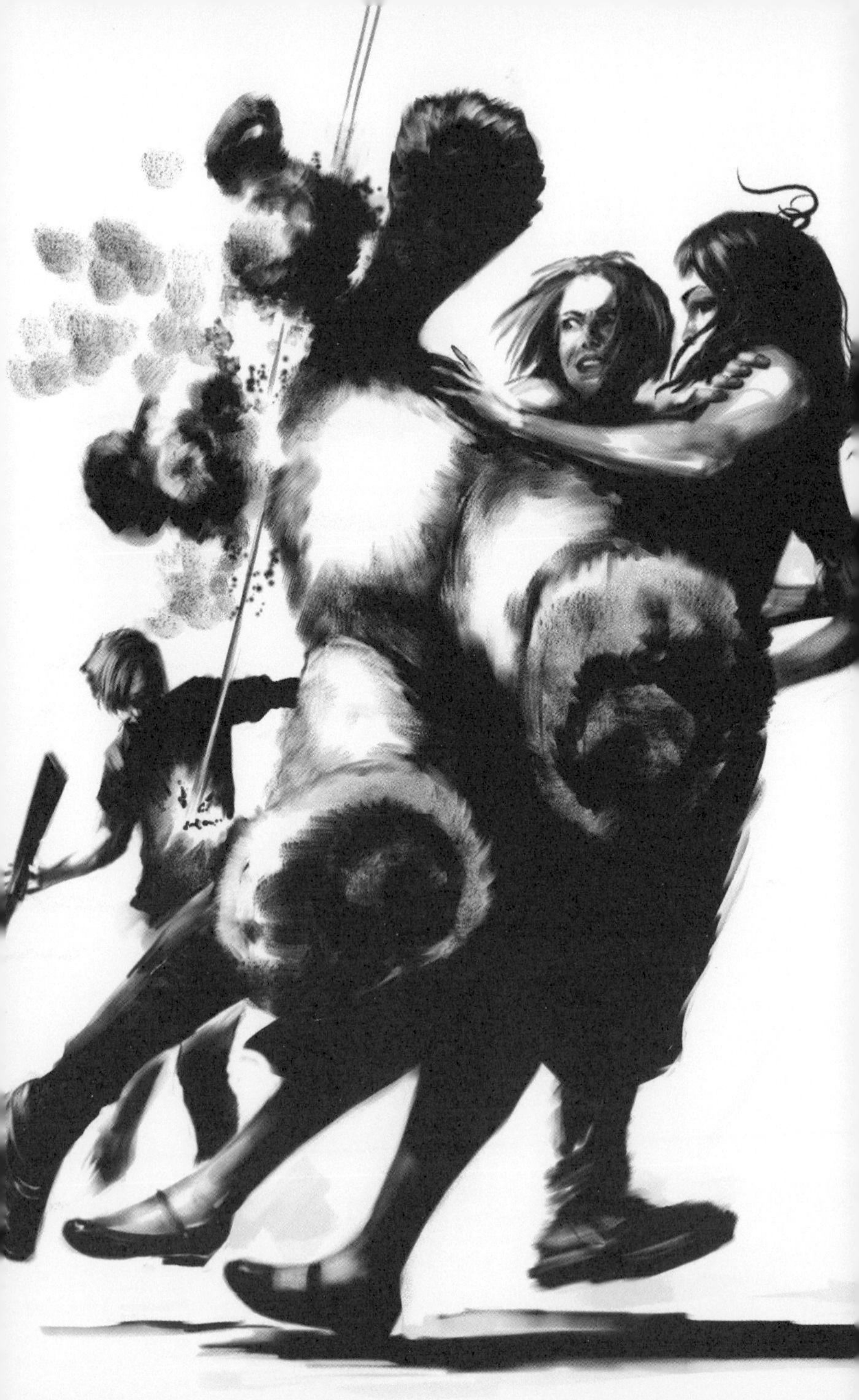

CHAPTER 6
BAIT

Kasia reacted first. She shoved Pandora aside.
Not a second too late.

A bullet ripped through the head of the
teddy bear she was holding. Stuffing exploded
into the air like snowflakes.

The bullet carried on and hit Jeff. He
doubled over, clutching his bleeding belly, and
screamed. Troy shielded Pandora with his body
and rushed her into the cover of the shooting
gallery. They huddled there with Kasia, Lennox,
Joe and Azumi all forming a protective shield
around Pandora.

"Where's the sniper?" Kasia said.

"I've no idea," Troy replied. His eyes darted from the big wheel to the bumper cars to the helter-skelter. Families and children still strolled around the funfair, unaware of the attack.

Jeff dropped to his knees, his screams lost among the joyful cries of the kids on the rides.

"Save my Jeffrey!" Troy heard Jeff's mother wail. She cowered behind the candy floss stall with her daughter clasped in her arms, her dead husband only a few metres from her.

Jeff collapsed and one of the armed bodyguards rushed out to drag him to safety. As he reached the boy, a gunshot rang out. The bodyguard was blown off his feet, dead before he even hit the ground.

Now people began to notice the three bullet-stricken bodies. Panic spread like a tidal wave through the funfair. The chaos made it even more difficult to lead Pandora to safety.

"We have to get out of here. We're sitting ducks!" Kasia said.

"We can't run until we know where the sniper is," Joe said. "Otherwise we could head directly towards the danger."

Jeff stretched out a hand to them and moaned, "*Help me ... please.*"

Pandora looked to Troy. "Save him!"

Troy hesitated. He shouldn't leave Pandora's side, not during an attack. But the pleading look in her eyes made him want to help. He rose to his feet.

"No!" Kasia said, and she grabbed Troy's arm. "The sniper's using him as bait to draw us out."

"I know," Troy said, "but at least I'm bulletproof."

Kasia didn't let go of his arm. "Pandora is your Principal, not Jeff."

"But we can't leave him to die," Troy argued.

But Kasia was firm. "Our only priority is Pandora's life," she said. "I'm team leader. Do as I say."

Another shot rang out and Jeff yelled in pain as a bullet blasted his leg.

"The sniper's *killing* him!" said Troy.

"Quiet!" Azumi snapped. She had her fingers on her temples as she focused hard. "Too many noises masking the gunshot ... but I think the sniper is somewhere high up ... in the direction of the bumper cars."

"Nice work, Bullet Ears!" Lennox said, and he peeked round the edge of the stall. "I can see the big wheel … the helter-skelter … and the house of horror."

"I'll need another shot or two to confirm," Azumi said.

"Jeff won't survive another shot!" said Troy.

Before Kasia could stop him, he sprinted out into no-man's-land and dived on top of the boy. A bullet struck Troy in the back. The impact felt like a battering ram. Troy groaned. He might be bulletproof, but every shot still hurt like hell.

From the cover of the shooting gallery, Lennox gave him a thumbs-up. "Good work getting the sniper to fire again!" he said with a grin. "Azumi's confirmed the location. It's the top of the helter-skelter."

Troy played dead, but he was able to look in the direction of the helter-skelter. A boy with spiked black hair came scooting down the slide. He was met at the bottom by a girl wearing a summer dress and white gloves. They seemed to have no idea of the danger they were in as they picked up the boy's backpack.

"RUN!" Troy shouted. He no longer cared if the sniper shot him again.

They both looked at him and surprise registered on their faces.

"GET OUT OF HERE! SNIPER!"

The girl grabbed the boy's hand and ran, disappearing among the panicked crowd.

"We're leaving, Troy," Kasia called. "Now!"

"Wait!" Troy cried. They knew where the sniper was located, but Troy realised they were still pinned down. The helter-skelter was in the middle of the funfair with 360 degree views. The sniper would have a clear shot whatever direction they ran.

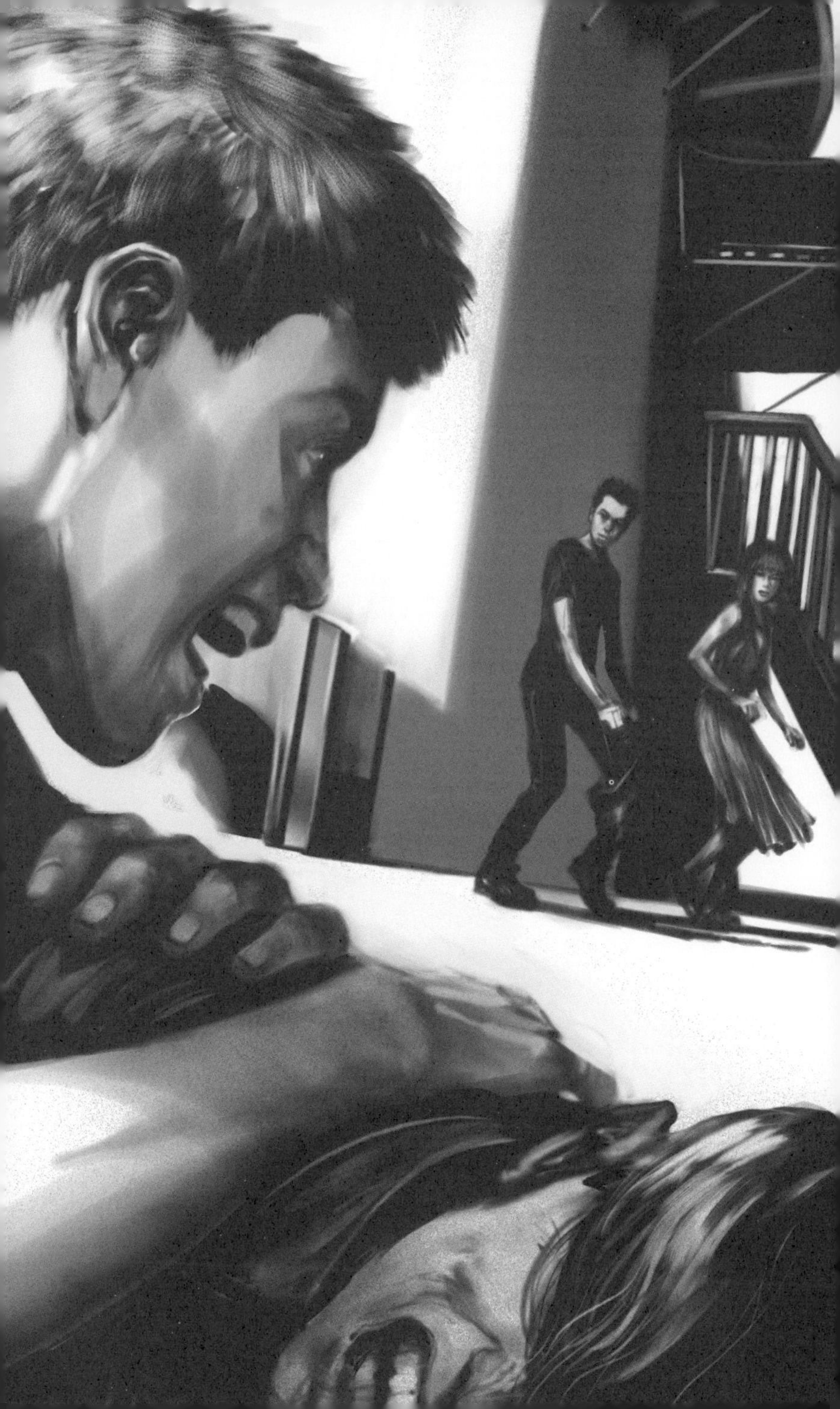

Troy spotted a canister strapped to the dead bodyguard's utility belt. A tear gas grenade.

They couldn't see the sniper. But what if the sniper couldn't see them either?

Troy reached out and tugged the canister free, pulled the pin and dropped it in front of him. Billowing clouds of white gas filled the air. Troy spluttered and his eyes stung as he got to his feet and dragged the injured Jeff to the shooting gallery. Lennox slung the boy over his shoulder. Together they fled the funfair, the smoke screen covering their escape.

CHAPTER 7
UNBROKEN SHIELD

Medusa strode into the briefing room, a scowl on her lean face. "The sniper got away," she said.

Troy coughed. "*How?*" His throat was still sore and his eyes red from the effects of the tear gas.

Medusa shrugged. "Your guess is as good as mine. A SWAT team rushed the helter-skelter soon after you left. But all they found was a single shell casing stuck in the floor. Forensics are trying to trace the bullet to the gun, but they're not holding out much hope for a match."

"Any news on Jeff?" Lennox asked. His T-shirt was still stained with the boy's blood.

"He's in intensive care," Medusa replied, "but the doctors are confident he'll survive. Troy, that was a brave act of yours."

"And stupid!" Kasia muttered.

Troy frowned at her. "Why?"

"You put us all in danger … again!" she snapped.

"No, I didn't." The first time Pandora had been the victim of an attack, he'd failed to react. This time it seemed Kasia thought he'd over-reacted.

"You disobeyed my direct command!" Kasia said.

"There was a life at stake," Troy argued.

"Yes, Pandora's! And you risked it for that slimeball Jeff."

"Without the smoke screen, we wouldn't have –"

"That's enough!" Medusa said. "Troy, Kasia's right. Pandora must *always* be your first priority. And you need to obey the team leader. Pandora's safety relies on an unbroken shield. If one part of that shield is missing, then she is vulnerable. Understood?"

Troy nodded, and the movement made him wince. He had an unusually large bruise where the sniper's bullet had hit him. And it seemed to hurt more than the other times he'd been shot. He guessed the sniper had been using an ultra high-powered rifle. In future he'd try to avoid bullets rather than catching them!

"With the sniper still at large, you'll all need to stay sharp at tomorrow night's Concert for Climate Change," Medusa went on. "The mayor is determined these attacks will not disrupt the city. He says that climate change is too important an issue to cancel the concert."

"Is Pandora still going?" Azumi asked.

Medusa nodded. "She's as stubborn as her father. Besides, all the big names will be there, including the four surviving members of the Council. Security will be tight. But this sniper seems to relish such a challenge."

CHAPTER 8
BLACKOUT

A battalion of photographers were pointing cameras like guns at the celebrities as they arrived at the concert. Movie stars, fashion models, musicians and business gurus had all turned up to support the mayor's Concert for Climate Change. Flashes lit up the night in blinding bursts as each guest paraded along the red carpet and was interviewed by various news channels.

Troy escorted Pandora along the wide path of carpet towards the concert hall. He wore sunglasses to reduce the glare from the camera flashes. He didn't want to be blinded and fail to spot a threat in the crowd.

Azumi didn't have that problem of course. Her Blindsight allowed her to move freely without the need to see, and her talent meant her other senses were more attuned to danger. She followed behind them, with an usher's badge pinned to her jacket.

Pandora stopped to answer a reporter's questions.

"After the tragic events at the funfair," the woman began, "aren't you scared to come out in public?"

"Of course I am," Pandora replied. "But I'm not going to let these terrorists win. After all, we're trying to save the planet here."

"Do you feel your father's doing enough to protect you?" the reporter asked.

Pandora nodded. "He's hired the best security for me."

"But I don't *see* any bodyguards," the reporter said, with a glance around.

Troy tried not to smile as the reporter looked right past him. With the focus on the future, young people had been invited to the concert too, so none of the bulletcatchers looked out of place on the red carpet.

"That's what makes them so effective," Pandora replied, before she walked off.

As he shadowed Pandora, Troy spotted Joe on the steps to the concert hall. He was scanning the crowd, memorising faces and identifying potential suspects. Kasia and Lennox were close by, mingling with the other guests.

Over their heads was the constant buzz of drones.

Troy glanced up. He hadn't forgotten his lesson from the Reactor Room – don't just search for the obvious threat and always look up. The drone squad criss-crossed the sky like hawks, their cameras spying on everyone and everything. Guards were stationed on all the rooftops. Police had searched the surrounding buildings. And massive floodlights lit up the city square. Every eye and ear of the Council Security Force was focused on the area of the concert hall.

There was no way on earth a sniper could get close without being detected.

Now they had been given the all-clear by security, the four surviving councillors arrived in limos with their families and made their way up the red carpet to join Mayor Lomez at the entrance to the concert hall.

"Azumi, any visions?" Kasia asked over their earpieces.

"Negative," Azumi replied. "But it's odd. It's all dark."

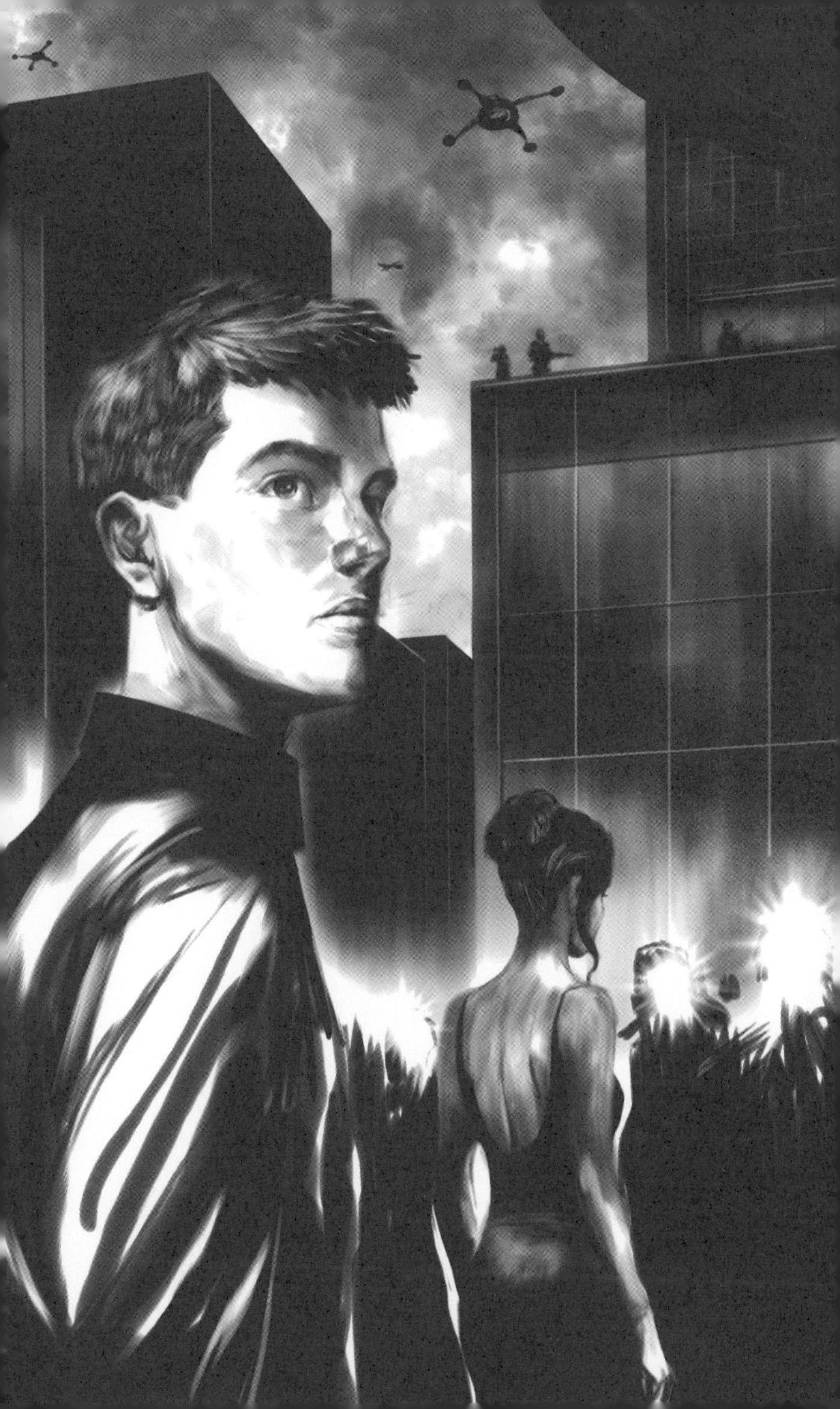

Pandora stopped for a row of photographers desperate to get a picture of her in the stunning red dress she wore. Troy was taken aback by how similar it was to the one her avatar had worn in the Reactor Room simulation. A shudder of unease ran down his spine as he recalled how *that* scenario had ended.

As they climbed the steps with the other guests, the spotlights on the concert hall went out. A moment later the street lamps died. Then the floodlights short-circuited in a dramatic burst of sparks.

A blackout engulfed the city for several blocks.

A murmur of surprise rippled through the crowd. The square was pitch-black.

"Pandora, are you still with me?" Troy asked, reaching out for her.

"Yes," she replied.

Then someone cried out in pain.

A camera flash went off. Then another. The strobe effect of the multiple flashes that followed was eerie. As if in slow motion, Troy watched one of the councillors tumble down the steps. Blood splattered across his white tuxedo.

His wife screamed. Then a second councillor fell. Shot through the heart. A bloody hole in her evening gown. The moment caught in a brief white flash.

The darkness returned and Kasia's voice barked in Troy's earpiece – "Protect Pandora!"

CHAPTER 9
BLOOD

Like everyone else Troy was blind in the
blackout. But his hand found Pandora's arm
and he wrapped himself around her. So did
Kasia and Lennox. They rallied to Troy's cry to
form a body-shield for the mayor's daughter.

Azumi gripped Troy's arm. "Follow me," she
said.

Azumi was not affected by the blackout, of
course, and she led them between the huddles
of terrified guests, up the steps and towards
the safety of the foyer of the concert hall.

As she guided them through the mayhem, someone yelled in pain and they heard the *thump* of another body slumping to the ground.

Troy realised the sniper could be anywhere in the darkness. Among the photographers. In a nearby building. Even ten blocks away! All the sniper needed was an infra-red night-scope to pick off his targets one by one.

Suddenly a bullet hammered Troy in the side. He stumbled under the impact, tripping up the others. Pandora let out a cry as the four of them hit the pavement. A bullet pinged off the ground, centimetres from Troy's head.

"Keep moving!" Azumi urged. She dragged Troy to his knees. "You OK?"

"I'll live," Troy groaned as he fumbled in the dark to find Pandora again.

Emergency lighting blinked on around the square as the generators kicked in. The scene was one of sheer chaos and panic. The people in the crowd were either fleeing or cowering from the unseen shooter. Two of the councillors had been shot dead. A third was dying and the fourth seriously injured. Mayor Lomez was safely buried beneath a squad of his own bodyguards ... but his daughter lay beside Troy in a pool of blood.

"No!" Troy cried. He frantically looked for her wound.

"I thought *you* were bulletproof," Pandora said. She pointed at a red stain on Troy's shirt.

"I am," Troy replied, ignoring the pain in his side. "It's your blood."

Pandora checked herself. "But I haven't been shot."

That's when Troy saw Kasia ... lying on the ground, not moving.

CHAPTER 10
FACE I.D.

Lennox gently shook her arm. "Kasia?"

Kasia rolled onto her back. Blood flowed from a small round hole in her chest. She might have the Reflex talent, but if she couldn't see the bullet coming, then she couldn't avoid it.

Troy put his hands to the wound and applied steady pressure to stem the bleeding.

Kasia groaned and her eyes flickered open. "*Pandora's ... priority*," she gasped, and a trickle of blood oozed from her mouth.

"Pandora's fine, but we need to get you to a hospital," Troy told her.

"I'm … team leader … do as I say."

Troy ignored her. He and Kasia might have their differences but he wasn't going to let the sniper use her as bait. He kept his hands over the wound as Joe ran over and assessed her condition.

"Bullet wound. Lower chest. High likelihood of critical internal injuries and organ trauma. Chance of survival … less than 15%."

"Then there's a chance," Troy replied.

"Pandora's survival is at 50% but dropping the longer we stay in the open," Joe went on.

"Kasia's orders – we evac Pandora *now*," Azumi stated, as she helped the mayor's daughter to her feet.

"I'm second-in-command," Troy reminded them as Kasia passed out with pain. "So I make the decisions now. We're *not* leaving her."

"We don't have time to argue," Lennox grunted as he lifted the lifeless Kasia onto his back. "Let's go."

The four bulletcatchers ran in a 'closed box' around Pandora. They crossed the concert hall's plaza and crashed through the doors into the foyer. Once they were inside, they took shelter behind a pillar. Lennox laid Kasia on the carpet and reapplied pressure to her wound. Azumi and Troy kept guard over Pandora, while Joe called for emergency back-up.

"Extraction vehicle three minutes out," Medusa replied from HQ into their earpieces. "Stay put until arrival."

Troy peered out of the foyer's doors. "Any idea where the sniper is?" he asked Azumi.

She shook her head. "I couldn't pinpoint the gunshots with all the noise."

"I did," Joe said. "During the blackout there was a muzzle flash from the hotel opposite."

Troy looked across the square. The high-rise luxury hotel must have had over 500 rooms. There was no way of telling which one held the sniper. "But which room?" he asked.

"With any luck the next shot will give his exact location away," Azumi said.

As they waited for the sniper to strike, Troy spotted a boy leaving the hotel entrance.

"Joe!" Troy said. "I need a Face I.D. Haven't we seen that boy with the skater backpack before?"

With his photographic memory, Joe only needed a single glance. "Affirmative," he said. "He was at the funfair."

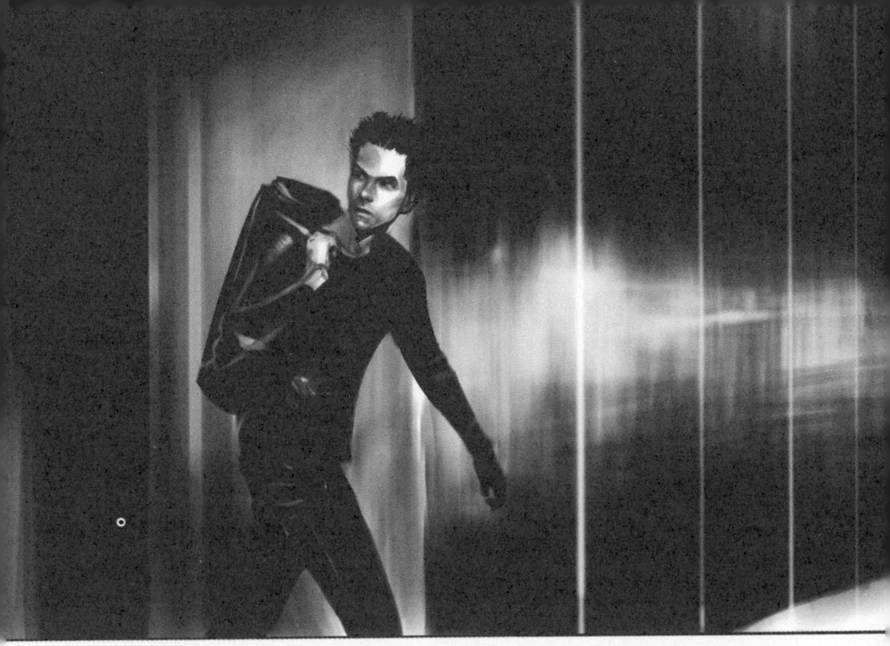

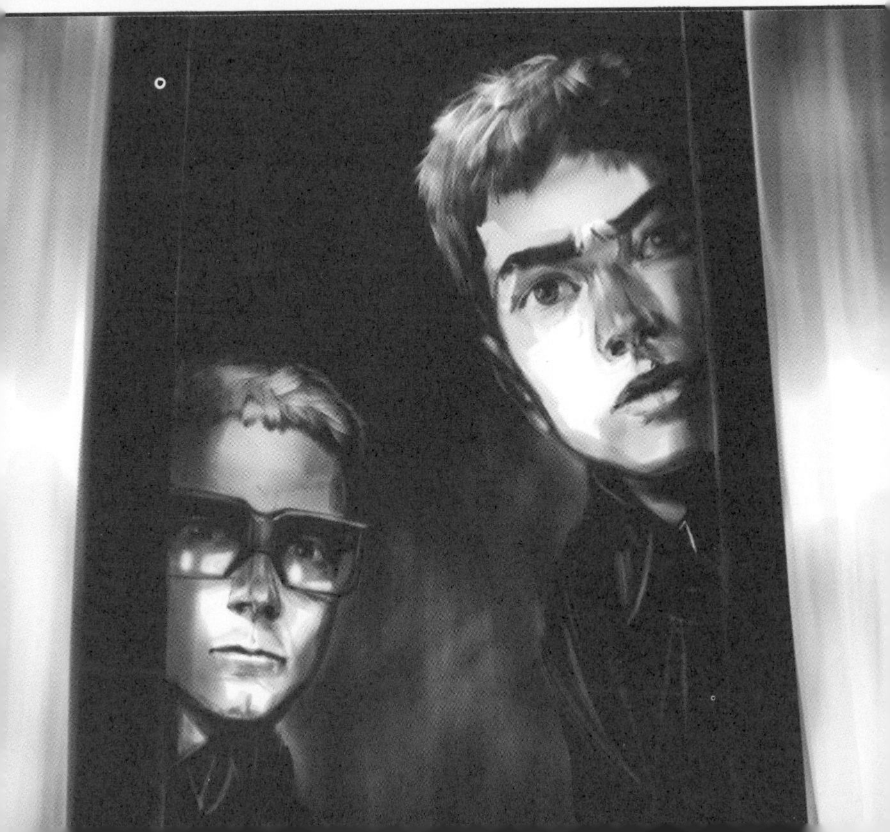

CHAPTER 11
SUBWAY

The presence of the spiky-haired boy from the helter-skelter was too much of a coincidence for Troy. He had to be connected with the sniper somehow – a spotter or a flanker to the shooter himself. Troy rose to his feet.

"Where are you going?" Joe asked.

"*When the battle is over, keep one hand on your sword*," Troy replied. "This battle isn't over – and it won't be unless we catch that sniper."

"Medusa told us to stay put," Azumi said.

"But this might be our only chance to –"

"We're losing Kasia!" Lennox interrupted. His hands were soaked with her blood.

"Where's the extraction team?" Troy cried in frustration and horror.

"One minute," came Medusa's reply. "Trauma kit in back seat."

Two blacked-out bulletproof SUVs screeched round the corner and across the square. Paying no heed to pedestrians, they mounted the kerb and drove up the ramp to the concert hall's front plaza. The first one picked up Mayor Lomez and roared away. The second waited for Pandora.

Troy and Azumi kicked open the foyer doors and bundled Pandora into the back seat. Lennox followed with Kasia in his arms. Joe jumped in and set to work right away with the trauma kit.

"Come on, Troy!" Azumi said as she climbed into the front passenger seat.

Troy shook his head. "I'm going after the boy. He could lead us to the sniper."

"*Don't* break up the shield," Azumi warned.

"We won't need a shield if the terrorists are captured," Troy argued.

"I've a bad vision about this," she said. "Troy, stay!"

Troy ignored her warning and turned to Pandora. "I have to do this ... for you and Kasia."

"I know," Pandora said, taking hold of his hand. "Just don't get yourself killed."

"No chance of that," he replied with a strained smile. "I'm bulletproof, remember!"

Troy closed the door and the SUV shot away with a squeal of tyres. His last glimpse of Kasia was her deathly pale face. Joe was inserting a blood pack into her arm as Lennox gave her CPR. Troy prayed to God she'd survive.

As the SUV disappeared down the road, Troy raced off in the opposite direction. He'd seen the boy head south down Main Street. Troy weaved in between the crowds of people, press and police. As he ran, his side throbbed from the impact of the sniper's bullet. It felt like he had a cracked rib.

The crowd thinned the further Troy got from the main square and he increased his pace. Ahead he spotted a boy with a backpack turn into a side street. Troy sprinted after him. Apollo's fitness regime gave him the burst of speed he needed to catch up. Troy rounded the corner, and thought for a moment he'd lost the boy. The street was deserted. Then he caught a glimpse of black spiky hair disappearing down a subway entrance.

Troy dashed across the street and down the steps. According to the sign across the entrance, the station was closed for repair. But the gate itself was unlocked. Troy slipped inside and entered the ticket hall. Only emergency lighting lit the space, giving the subway a creepy atmosphere.

The boy was nowhere to be seen. But Troy heard footsteps echoing down the static escalator. He followed the sounds. At the bottom Troy stepped onto a deserted platform. He looked around and listened for any sign of the boy.

In the gloom Troy heard the unmistakable click of a rifle being chambered.

CHAPTER 12
SHOCK TO THE SYSTEM

Only now did Troy realise how foolish he had been. The boy had led him to the sniper. But also into a trap ...

Troy turned to confront his fate. The slim black barrel of a collapsible stealth rifle was aimed at his chest. But Troy was more shocked by who was holding the deadly weapon.

"*You're* the sniper?" he said in disbelief.

The spiky-haired boy smirked. Close up, his eyes were coal-black and oddly large. "And you're hard to kill," he said. "I've shot you twice. But this time you'll stay dead."

Troy held up his hands.

"Too late to surrender," the boy sniper said, and his finger curled around the trigger.

Before the boy could fire, Troy grabbed the rifle's barrel in one hand and deflected the line of fire away from himself. A bullet bounced off the subway walls. Then Troy stepped forward and palm-struck the boy in the nose. Stunned, the boy put up little resistance as Troy twisted the rifle out of his grip. Troy then swung the gun butt around, and caught the boy hard in the jaw.

A perfect weapon disarm.

'Action beats reaction every time,' Troy thought as the boy dropped to the floor.

He shouldered the rifle, reloaded, then aimed it at the dazed sniper.

"You're coming with me," he said, and he waved the barrel in the direction of the stairs.

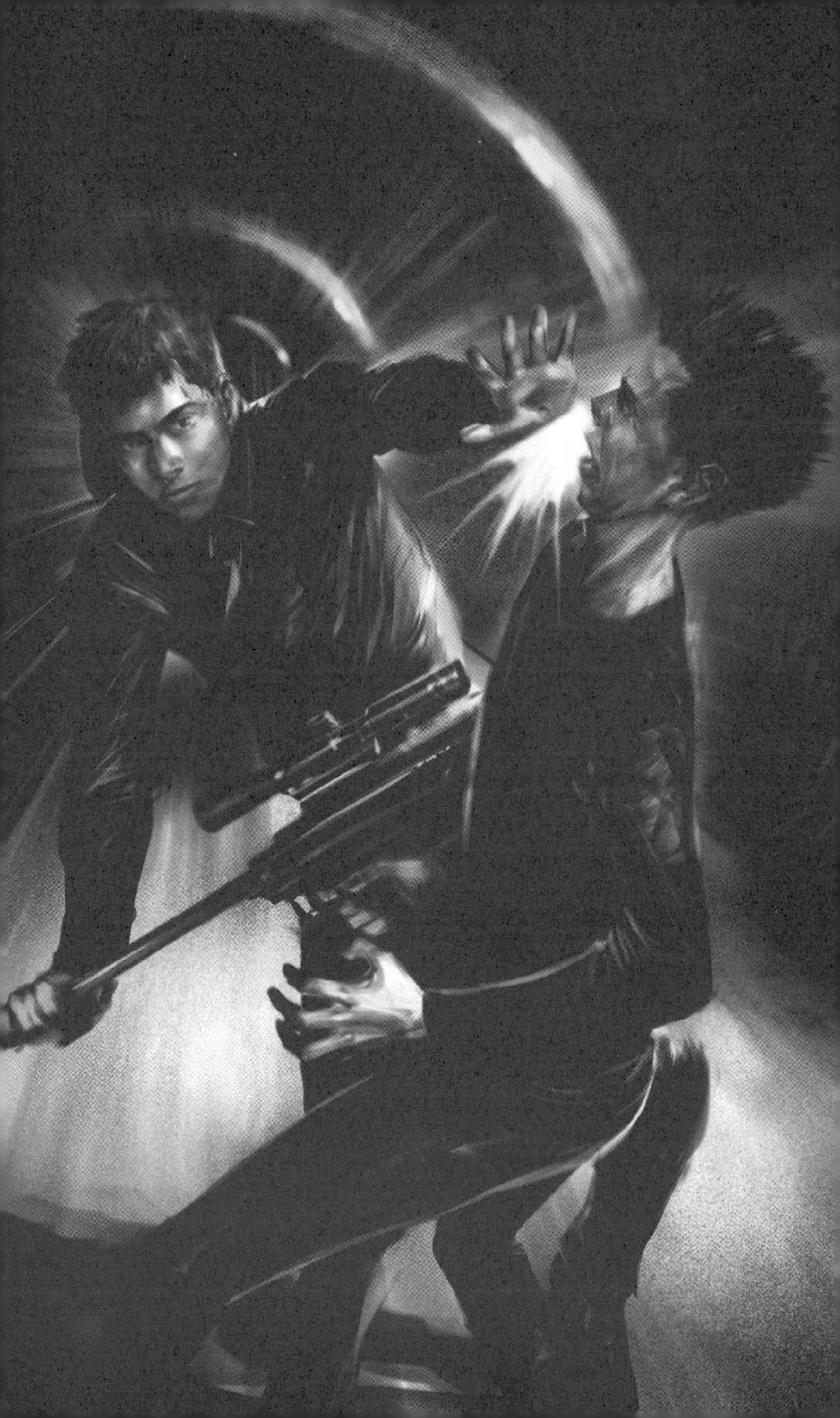

"Am I?" the boy replied. A look of defiance sparked in his round black eyes.

The lights overhead flickered. All of a sudden Troy felt as if he'd been struck by a bolt of lightning. His muscles locked out, his body jerked uncontrollably and he collapsed.

The boy stood up, rubbed his bruised jaw and calmly retrieved his rifle.

"Nobody touches *my* gun," he said, and spat onto Troy's face.

Troy lay helpless on the cold hard floor, his muscles twitching. The shock to his system had paralysed him. "What ... have you done to me?" he gasped.

"Me? Nothing," the boy replied with a grin. "That's all my sister's handiwork."

A girl stepped out from the shadows. She had black hair, deep purple at the tips. Troy recognised her as the girl with white gloves from the funfair.

"You don't believe bulletcatchers are the only talented ones round here, do you, Troy?" she said, as she strode over to him. She wore studded leather ankle boots and a matching black leather jacket.

"Who are you?" Troy said, as the pain in his muscles slowly eased.

"Well, you've met my brother Eagle Eye," she said. "With vision eight times stronger than any human, he can spot a target over two miles away – and he never misses."

She held up a bare hand and wiggled her slim fingers. Blue sparks crackled between them. "My name's Tricity."

Troy's eyes widened in fear. "Electricity! *That's* your talent?"

Tricity nodded. "Like an electric eel. I can generate, store and channel high-voltage strikes to knock out my prey ... or to kill them."

Troy felt the hairs on the back of his neck rise. The air around him grew super-charged. "*You're* the terrorists attacking our city?"

Tricity frowned. "I'm a fighter for the Army of Freedom, if that's what you mean."

"B ... But you're my age. You can't be terrorists."

"Why not? You're a bulletcatcher," she replied. "SPEAR have got you risking your life for spoilt rich kids. We're fighting for a far better cause. Freedom."

"But you're killing innocent people!" Troy argued. His strength was returning now.

"No one's innocent in this city." Tricity sneered. "They're all sinners. And in a war for freedom, sacrifices must be made."

Troy felt his jaw tighten in rage. That was the exact same phrase the terrorist who'd murdered his parents had used to justify his actions.

"I blacked out the city square," Tricity said with a smug smile. "That's a lot of juice for me to absorb in one go. And I need to offload some of it …"

She reached out her hand towards Troy's heart. The air crackled and hissed with sparks.

"You may be bulletproof, Troy," she said, grinning, "but you're not shock-proof!"

CHAPTER 13
THE VERDICT

"STOP!" A rasping voice echoed through the subway.

Tricity scowled but lowered her hand at the order. Out of a dark tunnel a black-and-white mask floated towards them. Then a tall man in a long black robe appeared and mounted the platform.

"I am judge, jury and executioner," he said. "Only I can decide his fate."

Tricity stepped back with a bow as The Judge strode over to them. He gazed down at Troy with his awful smiling-teardrop mask. A chill shuddered along Troy's spine. It was as if he had come face-to-face with the devil.

"Are you a sinner, Troy?" The Judge asked. "Or do you believe?"

"I ... I believe in good," Troy replied.

"And are you on the side of good?"

"Yes."

The Judge gave a cold laugh. "Then you are misled."

"No, *you* are the one who's deluded!" Troy shot back.

"Am I?" The Judge snapped. "I thought you were bulletproof."

"I am," Troy replied.

"Then why are you bleeding?" He pointed to Troy's side.

Troy looked down to where Eagle Eye's bullet had struck him. His shirt was sticky with fresh blood. Troy peeled back the material to see the bullet lodged in his side! It hadn't fully penetrated his body, but it had broken the skin. That at least explained the pain. But it didn't explain how such a thing could have happened.

Troy winced as The Judge prised the bullet from his flesh.

"It seems Medusa isn't telling you the whole truth," The Judge said, and he held the blood-stained bullet in front of Troy's eyes. "You now know my Army of Freedom have their own unique talents. But, by the looks of it, yours are fading."

All of a sudden Troy felt very vulnerable.

The Janus mask leaned in closer. "You should question who you are protecting and why," The Judge said.

"I *know* who I am protecting," said Troy.

"Do you?"

"Well, at least they're not hiding behind a mask like you!" Troy spat. "They're not the ones killing and spreading hate!"

"The Council is corrupt," The Judge said. "They and their families deserve to die."

"And what about people like my parents?" Troy cried, his hands clenched in fury. "Those people who've done nothing wrong?"

"Sacrifices for the greater good."

"And who judges *your* actions, Judge?" Troy demanded.

The terrorist leader looked upwards. "God will judge me. My mission is to rid this city of sin. And I will. With the Council all but gone, I only need to purge the mayor and his daughter."

"I'll never let that happen!" Troy said, rising to his feet. But before he could lash out at The Judge, he was stunned by a jolt of electricity.

As Troy quivered on the floor, Tricity asked, "What's your verdict, Judge? He's seen our faces. Knows who we are."

"You make a strong case," The Judge said. He raised a fist, with his thumb sticking out to the side. "My verdict is ..."

His thumb hovered.

Troy knew that whatever direction it went in would seal his fate.

The Judge turned his thumb down.

With a devilish grin Tricity thrust her open palm towards Troy's heart. A bolt of electricity burst out and Troy screamed as white-hot pain ripped through him.

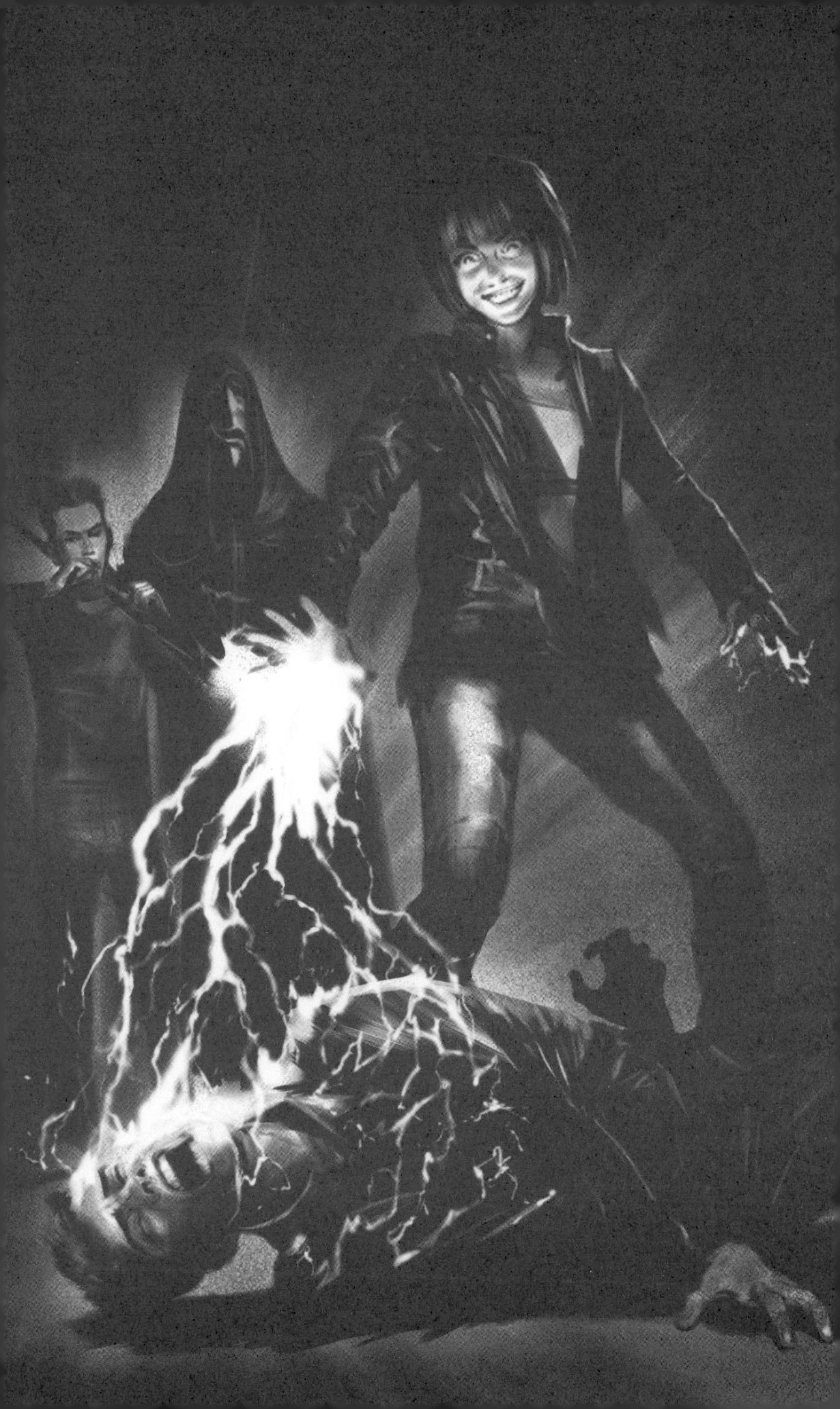

CHAPTER 14
DOUBT

Troy struggled to open his eyes against the blinding light. But when he did, he discovered Medusa standing by his bed in SPEAR's medical unit.

"How are you feeling?" she asked, dimming the glaring lights.

"Errr ... like I've been fried alive!" Troy mumbled. His mouth was dry and tasted of battery acid. A faint smell of burnt hair lingered in the air.

He sat up in bed, every muscle in his body tingling and sore. Lennox, Joe and Azumi greeted him with relieved smiles. "Where's Kasia?" he croaked.

His friends' smiles dropped and they exchanged sorrowful looks.

"Still in intensive care," Azumi replied. "Apollo has had to sedate her."

Troy closed his eyes again and tried to stop the tears that threatened to come.

"We found you on the street. Passed out," Medusa said. "What happened?"

Memories burst like exploding lightbulbs in Troy's head. He sat bolt upright. "The terrorists know about SPEAR!" he exclaimed. "They know we have talents! And they have talents too!"

Troy told them about his encounter with Eagle Eye and the boy's ultra-vision. Then about Tricity and her ability to conduct electricity.

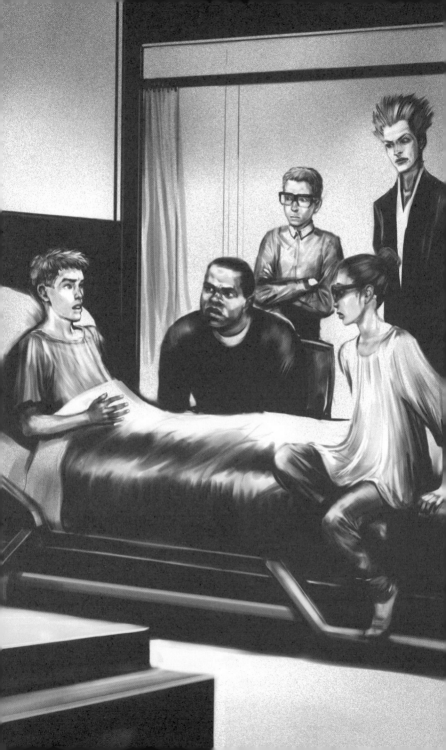

Medusa's eyes widened in shock. "That's beyond any power I've heard of. This changes everything."

"Where's Pandora?" Troy demanded. He tried to swing his legs out of bed but he had no strength. "The Judge has vowed to kill her and her father."

"Don't worry, she's at home," Medusa told him. She eased him back down on the pillow. "Their mansion is the most secure facility in all of Terminus City."

"Nowhere's safe," Troy said. "Not with the talents on the terrorists' side."

"Pandora will be safe as long as she has you as her bulletcatcher," Medusa assured him. "We'll get you back on duty as soon as you're fit. In the meantime, the rest of the team will provide round-the-clock protection."

Troy reluctantly gave in to her command. He was in no fit state to protect anyone.

Medusa and the others left him to recover. He lay immobile and stared at the ceiling. He had so many questions buzzing around his head.

How had he survived Tricity's attack?

Was Medusa hiding the truth from him?

Who was he really protecting?

And was it worth risking his life for?

The Judge had sown seeds of doubt in his mind.

But there was one question above all.

Troy lifted the bedsheet and checked the wound on his side. The blood had clotted and a scab was forming.

Was he was still bulletproof?

Our books are tested
for children and young people by
children and young people.

Thanks to everyone who consulted on
a manuscript for their time and effort in
helping us to make our books better
for our readers.